JASON STRANGE

23 CROW'S PERCH

Cover art by Alberto Dal Lago

Interior art by Nelson Evergreen

STONE ARCH BOOKS
a capstone imprint

Jason Strange is published by Stone Arch Books
A Capstone Imprint
1710 Roe Crest Dr.
North Mankato, Minnesota 56003
www.capstonepub.com

Copyright © 2012 by Stone Arch Books

Cataloging-in-Publication Data is available at the Library of Congress website.

ISBN: 978-1-4342-3297-7 (library binding)
ISBN: 978-1-4342-3885-6 (paperback)

Summary: Henry is a little creeped out by his new apartment. For one thing, the previous tenants died a few weeks before he moved in. For another, there's a gas leak somewhere in the building and the smell is starting to seep into his clothes. Just when Henry thinks things couldn't get much worse, one of the former tenants pays him a midnight visit . . .

Art Director: Kay Fraser
Graphic Designer: Hilary Wacholz
Production Specialist: Michelle Biedscheid

Photo credits:
Shutterstock: Nikita Rogul (handcuffs, p. 2); Stephen Mulcahey (police badge, p. 2); B&T Media Group (blank badge, p. 2); Picsfive (coffee stain, pp. 2, 5, 12, 17, 24, 30, 42, 48, 57); Andy Dean Photography (paper, pen, coffee, pp. 2, 66); osov (blank notes, p. 1); Thomas M Perkins (folder with blank paper, pp. 66, 67); M.E. Mulder (black electrical tape, pp. 69, 70, 71)

Printed in the United States of America in Stevens Point, Wisconsin.
102011   006404WZS12

TABLE OF CONTENTS

Chapter 1: Crow's Perch

Henry's mom was hauling a big box up the long flight of steps. Her brow was dotted with sweat and her jeans were dirty. Her hands were covered in grease from the tire she'd changed on the drive to Ravens Pass. Henry noticed a new tear on her left pant leg, too.

They both kept climbing until they reached the second floor. Then Mom dropped the box outside the door to apartment 23 and fished through her pocket for her keys.

Henry put down his box on top of the one his mom had been carrying. He pulled off his baseball cap and wiped his forehead with his sleeves. He leaned on the wall in the hall. "I just don't understand why Dad isn't here to help," Henry complained.

"Please, Henry," Mom said. "We've been over this. Dad has to work another ten days for his job or he won't get his severance pay."

"What's severance?" Henry asked.

Mom ignored him and kept looking for her keys. "I know they're in here someplace," she said. She dug deep into her bag. "At least, I think they are," she added quietly.

Henry sighed. He wasn't happy to be moving into this little, ratty apartment in Ravens Pass.

Just last week, his family was living in a big, beautiful house nearly a thousand miles away. Then Mom got a job transfer, so they all had to move. The company was paying the rent on this apartment until their family could get settled in a new house.

Finally Henry heard keys jingling. "Here they are," Mom said, pulling them out. She wiped her sleeve across her forehead and sighed. "This day might be improving."

Then she opened the door. Henry and Mom both immediately covered their noses and took a step back. The place stunk.

"Gross!" Henry said. "What is that smell?"

Mom shook her head and stepped slowly into the apartment. It was dark and dusty. The floors were filthy, the blinds were torn and cracked.

No matter where Henry went in the apartment, the awful smell invaded his nostrils.

"So much for the day improving," Mom said. She looked at Henry, still pinching her nose shut. "I don't suppose we can wait for Dad to get here next week, and let him do all the cleaning?"

Henry smiled and opened his eyes wide. "Maybe we can stay in a hotel until then?" he suggested.

Mom sighed. "I wish," she said. "But Ravencorp Enterprises isn't paying for a hotel stay."

Henry grunted. "This sucks."

"Tell me about it," Mom said, eyeing the dirty apartment. "Anyway, let's start cleaning."

Chapter 2: A Visitor

Henry and his mom cleaned silently for hours. They went through bottle after bottle of heavy duty cleaner, and roll after roll of paper towels. Mom used four sponges just to scrub out the inside of the fridge. When it was almost dark outside, Mom finally stopped.

"I have to get myself cleaned up," she said, wiping her brow. "I'm meeting Mr. Finch for dinner soon."

"Your new boss?" Henry asked.

Mom nodded. "Anyway, we've done a good job of cleaning," she said. "This place is almost livable. Let's call it a night."

* * *

An hour later, Mom had cleaned up and changed clothes. Henry watched from the apartment door as she left.

His mother waved. "Be good," she said over her shoulder.

Henry closed the door and walked to his room. His arms were sore from scrubbing floors and walls and counters all afternoon.

But despite all their effort, the horrible smell still saturated the air in the apartment. It wasn't as obvious as it had been at first, but that terrible stink still lingered beneath the scent of cleaners and laundry soap.

It probably didn't help that all the windows were stuck shut and refused to open, so Henry couldn't even air out the apartment. Exhausted and too frustrated to sleep, Henry walked to his bedroom.

As he entered his new room, Henry saw that there was more work to be done. His boxes and luggage were still packed, and his mattress was still bare. But he was too tired to care. Henry pulled off his hat, tossed it in the corner, and let himself fall hard onto the bare mattress. He stared out the window and watched the setting sun until his eyes grew heavy.

* * *

THUMP. Something fell. *Sounds like it came from the kitchen,* he thought. Then Henry heard the sound of running water.

Henry saw that the window was dark. *How long did I sleep?* he wondered. It was hard to think. His head ached, and his whole body felt warm.

Henry struggled to sit up. No curtain or blinds covered the window. Then he remembered where he was — not at home, but in the new, smelly apartment.

"Mom?" he called out. There was no answer. Henry rubbed his eyes. He was sure he'd heard her.

Henry had no idea what time it was. He looked around his room for his clock, but then he remembered it was still packed. He got to his feet and stumbled over to his jacket, which hung on the back of the door. He found his phone in one of the side pockets, but the battery was dead.

The lights in the hall were off, but a little light escaped from underneath the kitchen door. "Mom must already be home from dinner," Henry said to himself.

Henry yawned as he walked down the hall toward the kitchen. With one hand, he steadied himself along the wall on his right. When he reached the door, he slowly pushed it open. His mother was at the sink with her back to the door, wearing a bathrobe. The running water sent puffs of steam into the room, making it hard to see.

"Hi, Mom," he said, taking a seat at the small table against the wall. The table was green, old, and made of aluminum. Henry leaned his elbows on the table. It was ice cold. Henry wanted to rest his warm head on the cool surface. "Do we have any aspirin?" he asked. "I'm not feeling so great."

Mom didn't turn around or speak. Instead, she faced the sink, scrubbing away at something. Henry raised his eyes and glanced at her.

"Mom," Henry said, a little louder. She didn't flinch. Then Henry noticed something strange. The woman's hair was different somehow, and she was much more slender than Mom.

That's not her, Henry realized.

"Hey!" Henry said, getting up. His chair scraped across the floor, squealing loudly. "Who are you?"

At the sound of the chair, the woman's head moved slightly, and she shut off the water. At the same moment, Henry heard the front door's lock being opened, followed by the sound of his mother's high-heeled shoes clicking across the linoleum hall floor.

"Henry?" his mother called from the hallway. He heard the light click on.

"Who are you?!" Henry growled. He ran to the woman at the sink and angrily grabbed her by the shoulder. But when he tried to turn her around, her empty robe fell to the floor.

The woman was gone.

Chapter 3: Intruder

"Mom!" Henry called out.

Henry ran through the swinging door just as Mom reached the kitchen. Her bag of groceries fell to the floor, sending cans and apples flying everywhere.

"Henry!" she said, startled. "Why are you shouting?"

Henry grabbed her by the wrist and pulled her into the kitchen. "Look!" he said.

Henry pointed where the bathrobe had been. But as he turned around, he saw that it was gone.

"Look at what, Henry?" Mom asked. "Am I supposed to be seeing something?"

Henry scratched his head. "It was right there just a second ago," he said. He looked back at his mom and made eye contact with her. "I think our apartment is haunted, Mom."

Mom rolled her eyes. "Honestly, Henry," she said. "I realize you don't like it here, but I don't have time for your games right now. Just help me pick up the groceries and put them away. I'm dying for a shower and I'm about to fall asleep on my feet."

"But —" Henry began.

His mother cut him off. "*Now,* Henry."

Henry went into the hall. He picked up a couple of cans and set them on the kitchen table. He felt woozy — as if he were still half-asleep. "Maybe I dreamt it, or something," Henry said, "but I thought you were standing at the sink a few minutes ago."

"Well, I wasn't," Mom said. She put away the cans. "I was trying to say good night to the most boring man I've ever had dinner with."

"It was that bad?" Henry asked.

"Worse," Mom said.

"Then why did you take the job?" Henry asked.

Mom shook her head sadly.

"I didn't have much of a choice," Mom said. "With your dad's job ending, I couldn't say no. We need the money."

Henry nodded. "I guess," he said.

"I need to get ready for bed," Mom said. "You should finish unpacking."

* * *

Henry wandered into the dark living room. It was the only room they'd gotten set up before Mom left for supper.

He headed straight for the floor lamp in the corner and flipped the switch. It flickered on and off a couple of times before finally staying on. Even so, the light was very dim. Henry tapped the bulb with his fingernail and it got brighter for an instant, but it quickly darkened again.

"This apartment sucks," he said.

Henry turned on the TV. Static filled the screen.

"Great," he muttered. He dropped to his knees to find the cable hookup. The black cord was frayed and broken, and the bare wires stuck out from a connection in the wall. They were covered in cobwebs and dust. "So much for that," Henry said to himself, turning off the TV.

A unopened box of books sat next to the little couch. Henry tore off the top and poked around inside, hoping to find a comic book or two. Most of the old and dusty books were his mother's, but at the bottom he spotted what looked like one of his graphic novels. He pulled at the top books, but they wouldn't budge. He tugged and tugged at them until the box gave way, scattering thick little paperbacks all over the floor.

"This is not my night," Henry said.

Henry picked up most of the books, then leaned down to retrieve a few from under the coffee table. Just then, the lamp grew dim. Suddenly, it turned off.

"Oh, come on," Henry muttered. He groped blindly in the dark for the paperbacks under the table. Instead, he found a sneaker.

"I don't remember leaving any of my shoes in here," he said. When he grabbed it, he felt that it was wet and grimy. He pulled his hand back quickly. Then, Henry heard a soggy footstep, then another, move slowly across the thick living room carpet.

Henry tried to stand up and banged his head against the underside of the coffee table. He reached for the couch and got to his feet. "Who's there?" he asked, holding his head with one hand.

There was no response.

"Mom, is that you?" Henry asked.

But it wasn't. He could hear the shower still running down the hall.

A voice came from the darkness. "Who are you?" It sounded close. *Very* close.

"Who's there?" Henry asked. He moved away from the voice until he backed into the lamp. It flickered on for a brief moment, and Henry saw something. Some*one*. It was a boy about his age, or maybe a little older? Just then, the light cut out again.

"What's your name?" the boy whispered in the darkness. He seemed to be pleading. His voice sounded muffled, like it was up close but also far away at the same time. It sounded as dusty as Mom's old paperbacks.

Henry grabbed the lamp and shook it, hoping it would come back to life. A hand grabbed Henry's shoulder.

"Stop," the boy said. There was a hint of anger in his voice now. "What are you doing in my apartment?"

"Get away from me!" Henry shouted, still shaking the lamp. It flickered back on, spilling light across the room.

Henry spun to find himself face to face with the boy. His pale face was covered with dirt and insects and bits of mold. Henry pushed him away and the boy fell backward, hitting the wall with a loud, dull thud.

The boy clenched his teeth as he leaned against the wall. "Why did you do that?" he asked, rubbing his head.

Henry tried to answer, but couldn't.

The boy bared his teeth in anger. Henry could see that his lips were cracked, and several of his teeth had fallen out. An insect with many legs creeped out from between his lips, skittered down his chin, and crawled into one of the holes in his gums.

"WHY ARE YOU HERE?!" the boy growled.

Henry covered his face with his hands, dropped to his knees, and screamed.

Chapter 4: Fever

A hand grabbed his shoulder. "Henry," a voice said. "Henry, open your eyes."

"Get away from me!" Henry shouted.

"Henry!" The hand shook him and then released its grip.

"Stop!" Henry screamed. "Leave me alone!"

Henry slowly uncovered his eyes.

The lamp was brighter now. The creepy boy was nowhere to be seen.

"Henry," the voice said. Henry spun around in a panic. He looked up to see his mother standing over him. He took a deep breath and let it out slowly.

"Don't do that," Henry said. "You scared me."

Did I just dream all that? he thought, standing up. He felt dizzy.

"What were you yelling about just now?" Mom asked.

"I — I don't know," Henry said, breathing heavily. He tried to stand, but wobbled and sat down onto the couch.

Mom gently pressed her hand onto Henry's forehead. "I think you might have a fever," she said.

"I'm fine," Henry insisted. "I think I just had a nightmare."

Mom ruffled his hair. "You're probably exhausted, huh," she said. "I guess it's been a long day for both of us. You should get to bed. Tomorrow morning, I have to go to work — and *you* have to go down to the school to register as a new student."

"Ugh," Henry said. "Can't wait."

Henry could feel his mom's eyes following him as he staggered slowly down the hall to his bedroom. As he pushed open the door, it creaked loudly, as if it hadn't been opened in ages.

Henry dug through his bags until he found one of his comic books. He sat on the edge of his bed and tried to read, but his eyes started to feel heavy.

Henry let out a long sigh. Then, in one fluid movement, Henry grabbed his pillow and blanket, threw his comic book to the floor, and curled up on the bed. He fell asleep almost instantly, with the light still on.

Chapter 5: New Kid

The next day, Henry decided to walk to school. It wasn't very far from his apartment, and the walk would give him a chance to see his new hometown.

Ravens Pass was small and quiet. On the way to school, Henry passed the post office, the police station, and a pizza place. He only saw a handful of people the entire trip.

When he reached Ravens Pass Middle School, he approached the sign that read *OFFICE* and walked inside.

Henry opened his mouth to tell the secretary who he was, but the woman at the desk cut him off. "Are you a new student?" she asked. Henry nodded. "I see. Well, we're already over a month into the school year. You'll have a lot of catching up to do."

"What do you mean?" Henry asked. "I thought school didn't start for ten more days."

"I don't know where you're moving here from," the woman said. "But in this state, school began several weeks ago."

She smiled, then pushed a small stack of papers over the desk to him. "I need you to fill these out," she said. "And no hats in school, please."

Henry pulled off his baseball cap, folded it, and shoved it into his back pocket. Then he took the papers and a pen from a coffee mug filled with them.

"Are there any other new kids here this year?" Henry asked as he filled out the forms.

"We don't get many new students in Ravens Pass," the woman at the desk said. "Plenty of people move away, but almost no one moves in."

The woman stood, then went over to the automatic hole puncher on the wall.

"Why is that?" Henry asked. She didn't seem to hear the question over the thumping and clunking of the machine she was using.

Henry finished filling out the forms, so he waited for the woman to finish using the machine.

When she was finally done, she scooped up Henry's papers with a smile and looked over them quickly.

"Let's just make sure you didn't miss anything here," she said, flipping through the papers. As she read, her smile faded and her face went pale.

"You're living at 23 Crow's Perch?" she asked quietly.

Henry nodded.

"In the big brick apartment building?" she asked.

"Yes," Henry said. "Why? What about it?"

She looked at Henry and started to speak, but the phone rang. She turned and grabbed it. "Ravens Pass Middle School," she said into the phone. "This is Janice."

"Wait, what happened at 23 Crow's Perch?" Henry asked. But the woman put up her hand to silence him and turned away with the phone.

Henry glanced at the clock. He was already late for his first class, but now he felt like he needed to find out what was so weird about his apartment building.

When the secretary turned her back, Henry slipped out of the office and headed down the hall toward the library.

* * *

"Good morning," the librarian said when Henry walked in. The librarian was a tall young man with a dark beard. He sat behind a counter at a computer and didn't look up until he had finished typing.

"Shouldn't you be in class?" the librarian asked.

"Oh, I'm new here," Henry said. "The woman at the office didn't give me my schedule yet." That wasn't completely true, but Henry wanted to find some information about his apartment building. The library seemed like a good place to start.

"Right," the librarian said. "Then you should probably get back to the office to get your schedule, huh?"

"Yes sir," Henry said. "I just was hoping to find out what happened at 23 Crow's Perch. The secretary at the office got all weird when I told her it was my new address."

The librarian frowned. "You live there?" he asked.

Henry nodded.

FAMILY
OF TWO
FOUND
DEAD

Local businessman
found guilty of murder

After a brief moment, the librarian motioned to the chair next to him and said, "Sit down. You can read about it for yourself."

Henry sat down next to the librarian as he typed into an online news search. "Here it is," the librarian said. He gave Henry a nervous, sad sort of smile. "Take your time. I have some books to re-shelve." He stood and wheeled a book cart toward the back of the library.

Henry looked at the screen. The librarian had found an article from the local newspaper. The headline read *FAMILY OF TWO FOUND DEAD* in big, bold, letters. Right underneath, in smaller letters, it read *LOCAL BUSINESSMAN FOUND GUILTY OF MURDER.*

Henry scanned the article.

It had happened at his apartment building. In his apartment. A woman and her kid had recently moved into the apartment. Not long after, natural gas began to fill the apartment, quickly reaching toxic levels. Both were found dead the following week.

Henry kept reading. In the middle of the story, the paper said a local businessman named Jacob Finch was convicted for the two deaths. It turned out he had bought an unusually large life insurance policy for the woman, one of his employees. After her death, he would have collected millions of dollars of insurance money from the policy. Police speculated that the man planned to ignite the gas and kill the victims in a fire. However, before that happened, the two tenants died of asphyxiation in their sleep.

The librarian returned after a few minutes. Henry was a little creeped out by the idea of living in a dead family's apartment. "Can you print this for me?" he asked. "I think I should show my mom this article."

The librarian sighed. "I have to charge you a dollar because it's not for school," he said.

It's worth it, thought Henry. *If Mom knows about the apartment's history, maybe she'll let us move.*

Henry dug in his pockets for four quarters and handed them to the librarian.

"Okay," the librarian said. He walked over to the printer. It chugged and clunked, then spit out two pages. The librarian picked them up and turned toward Henry.

"Hey, what was the name of that businessman's company?" Henry asked.

The librarian handed him the papers. "Ravencorp Enterprises," he said. "Why?"

Ravencorp! Henry knew that name. That was the company that had just hired his mom.

Henry glanced down at the story in the printout, desperately searching for the name of the businessman. Two thirds of the way through the article, he found it: Jacob Finch.

That's the name of Mom's boss! thought Henry.

Henry released the printout from his grip and dashed toward the library's exit. He was out the doors before the papers even hit the floor.

"Hey, wait!" the librarian called after him, but Henry didn't hear. He wouldn't have stopped even if he had.

He's going to do it again, Henry thought. *Jacob Finch is going to kill my mom!*

- Chapter 6: Fear -

I have to warn my mother, Henry thought as he ran through the empty school hallway. A hall monitor called after him, but he just kept running.

A second later, Henry burst right through the front doors of the school and ran into the street. His feet slapped against the concrete loudly as he sprinted.

Henry didn't stop running until he reached the door to his apartment. Gasping for breath, he threw open the door. "Mom!" he called out, running inside. There was no answer, but that horrible smell was even stronger now. It hit him like a punch in the face, and now he recognized it: natural gas. There was something else, too — some kind of sickly sweet smell. But he could definitely smell gas.

Henry covered his face with the top of his shirt and ran through the apartment.

"Mom!" he called out. "You're not safe. We have to get out of here!"

The door to his mom's room was open a crack. The light was on and flickering. He pushed the door open and saw that the room was a complete mess. The mattress was half off the bed and didn't have any sheets.

The window was covered in dust and spider webs, like no one had been there for a long time.

As the light blinked off and on, shadows crossed the room in chaotic patterns. As the light flickered back on for a brief moment, Henry was sure he saw the strange woman from the kitchen lying on the mattress. Her eyes were open and her hair was wet. But when the lights flickered off, then on again, he saw that the mattress was empty.

Henry backed out of the room. In the corner of his eye, he caught a flash of light from the end of the hall. He turned to find the kitchen door swinging, as if someone had just gone inside.

Henry ran down the hall and into the kitchen. "Mom!" he cried. She had her back to him as she faced the sink.

Henry took a cautious step toward her.

"Mom . . . ?" he whispered.

She turned off the water and turned to face him. As she curled her lips into a smile, Henry felt sick. His mom's face looked like the face of the boy Henry had seen the night before: dirty and peeling. Decaying. A bug scurried out from her ear, across her cheek, and disappeared into her nostril.

"Henry," she whispered. Dust fell from her lips as she spoke.

Henry went pale. He took two steps back toward the door.

"Don't run, Henry," Mom begged.

Slowly, she reached out for him with both of her arms. Henry stumbled backward through the kitchen door and into the hall, horrified.

Then Henry turned and ran out the front door.

"Henry, come back!" she called after him. "Please don't leave me."

But Henry didn't turn around, and he didn't stop. He just ran. He didn't know where he was going, and he didn't care.

He just kept running.

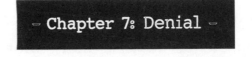

Chapter 7: Denial

Henry ran through a sleepy side street
of Ravens Pass and into the busier streets of
the business district. He dashed past the post
office toward the middle school. The sun was
bright — too bright. He felt like he had just
exited a dark movie theater and his eyes
couldn't get used to the light.

Henry ran as fast as he could, until his
legs ached and his lungs burned.

Just outside of the school, Henry saw a bench. A man was sitting on one end. He sat down on the other side so he could catch his breath and collect his thoughts.

Henry felt like crying, but didn't want a stranger to see him sobbing. That's when he looked at the man and realized who he was. The Ravens Pass Middle School librarian.

"Well, well," said the librarian. "A few hall monitors are looking for you, young man."

"Oh," Henry said, startled. "Sorry about that. I . . . I wanted to find my mom. To warn her."

"Warn her?" the librarian asked. He pulled out a sandwich from his shoulder bag, unwrapped it, and took a bite. "About what?"

Henry did his best to pull himself together. "That gas leak and insurance scam," he said. "My mom is . . . working for Ravencorp Enterprises."

The librarian wrinkled his forehead. "That can't be right," he said. "The boss of Ravencorp is in jail. I don't think the company even exists anymore."

"What do you mean?" Henry asked.

"I mean Ravencorp Enterprises went out of business," the librarian said. "Mr. Finch, the head of Ravencorp Enterprises, is in prison. He's serving back-to-back life sentences."

Henry shook his head. "That's impossible," he protested. "Mr. Finch just hired my mom. She had dinner with him last night. She starts working for him tomorrow."

"Not possible," the librarian mumbled, his mouth full of peanut butter and jelly. "Last month, when the woman's husband arrived in town, he found both of them dead. Poor man. His kid was supposed to start school here a couple of days before they found him."

"What date did this happen?" Henry asked.

The librarian tapped his chin. "This would have been September . . . 23rd, I think," he said. He nodded once. "Yes, it was the 23rd. It was kind of a big deal around town, actually — everyone was talking about it. Nothing like that has ever happened here before."

Henry shook his head. "You're wrong," he said. "Today is September 23rd. October isn't even here yet!"

Henry pulled out his phone and held it up, showing the librarian the date. "See?"

The man squinted at the phone. "Yeah, that says September 23rd, but it's wrong," he said. "Today is the 23rd of October. Your phone must be broken, or something."

"No way," Henry said. "I know it's still September. My dad is coming to town on September 27th and he isn't even here yet!"

The librarian tapped his chin with his finger. Then he turned away from Henry and grabbed a newspaper from his shoulder bag. "Here," he said, smiling. He pointed at the top of the front page. "See that? October 23rd is today's date."

Henry stared blankly at the paper. His shoulders sank low, and the remaining color in his face faded.

The librarian folded up the paper and stood. "Now you'd better get back to school," he said. "And you might want to stop by the nurse's office on the way. You look a little pale."

Then the librarian walked away, leaving Henry all alone.

- Chapter 7: Acceptance -

Henry lurched back toward home. He moved slowly, exhausted by everything that had happened that day. His mind felt clouded and confused.

Before Henry knew it, he was pulling himself up the railing of Crow's Perch and up the stairs toward his apartment.

Henry groaned. Climbing the steps felt impossible.

Henry found it difficult to even take a deep breath. His feet felt heavy, like his shoes were wet with mud. By the time he reached the second floor, they felt like cement.

The door to his apartment was open a little. He realized he hadn't closed it when he had run off earlier in the day. A thin stream of light cast the entrance in an eerie glow.

As Henry pushed the door open with his shoulder, the smell hit him at once. But this time, he didn't bother to cover his nose. He inhaled deeply, as if able to breathe for the very first time. He headed straight for the source of the smell, the kitchen.

Henry walked down the long main hall. The lights flickered overhead. The walls were dirty and stained. It looked as if he and his mom had never even cleaned them.

He swung open the door. Mom was sitting at the table.

Mom's face was ragged and peeling. She looked up and smiled sadly as Henry walked in. He sat down across from her.

Between them was the newspaper from September 23rd. It was the same article that Henry had read in the library.

Henry's face itched. He lifted his hand to his cheek and felt that the skin was dry and peeling, just like his mother's. His nose was decaying too.

As his fingers traced slowly across his face, Henry felt exposed bone along his jawline. He looked at his hands. His fingernails were yellow, dirty, and cracked. Dried blood filled the corners of his nails where they met his fingers.

The woman across the table took his hand and held it in hers. They were as dry as bone.

"Don't run away again, Henry," she said. "Please don't leave me all alone."

Henry picked up the newspaper. "It's us," he said. "The mom and the son who died here . . . we're them."

His mother nodded and smiled. Her eyes wrinkled like she might cry, but she couldn't. She had no tears left.

"I know, sweetie," she said. "I know."

Case number: 232977

Date reported: November 30

Crime scene: Crow's Perch apartment building, apartment 23

Local police: None

Victims: Henry Stark, age 14; Melanie Stark, age 36

Civilian witnesses: Damon Crick, landlord of Crow's Perch apartment building

Disturbance: Crick filed a report claiming to have seen the ghosts of two former residents, Henry Stark and his mother, Melanie Stark. The Ravens Pass Police Department passed the case along to me.

CASE NOTES:

MR. CRICK GAVE ME A PICTURE OF HENRY STARK AND LED ME TO APARTMENT 23. HE REFUSED TO GO INSIDE HIMSELF. I DIDN'T HAVE TO WAIT LONG TO SEE WHY.

THE KITCHEN LIGHTS FLICKERED ON, THEN OFF, THEN ON AGAIN. EVERY TIME THE LIGHTS DIMMED, I SAW TWO PEOPLE SITTING AT THE KITCHEN TABLE, THEIR HANDS INTERTWINED, THEIR HEADS HUNG LOW AND SAD.

I MOVED CLOSER. THE LIGHT SWITCHED OFF ONCE MORE, AND THERE THEY WERE AGAIN. THIS TIME, THE LIGHT STAYED OFF. I STARED AT THE BOY. THERE WAS NO DOUBT ABOUT IT — DESPITE THE ADVANCED LEVEL OF FACIAL DECAY, HE WAS DEFINITELY HENRY STARK.

HENRY SLOWLY TURNED HIS HEAD TOWARD ME. AT THAT MOMENT, THE ROOM FILLED WITH THE SMELL OF GAS. IT GREW SO COLD THAT I COULD SEE MY BREATH. AS HIS EYES LOCKED ONTO MINE, I FELT A TIGHTNESS IN MY NECK, AS IF INVISIBLE HANDS WERE WRAPPED AROUND IT. HENRY WHISPERED, "LEAVE US ALONE."

I LEFT, INTENT ON DOING JUST THAT. I MADE A FEW CALLS AND HAD THE ENTIRE BUILDING CONDEMNED. TWO DAYS LATER, I NAILED THE BOARDS UP MYSELF.

DEAR READER,

THEY ASKED ME TO WRITE ABOUT MYSELF. THE FIRST
THING YOU NEED TO KNOW IS THAT JASON STRANGE IS
NOT MY REAL NAME. IT'S A NAME I'VE TAKEN TO HIDE MY
TRUE IDENTITY AND PROTECT THE PEOPLE I CARE ABOUT.

YOU WOULDN'T BELIEVE THE THINGS I'VE SEEN, WHAT I'VE
WITNESSED. IF PEOPLE KNEW I WAS TELLING THESE STORIES,
SHARING THEM WITH THE WORLD, THEY'D TRY TO GET ME TO
STOP. BUT THESE STORIES NEED TO BE TOLD, AND I'M THE
ONLY ONE WHO CAN TELL THEM.

I CAN'T TELL YOU MANY DETAILS ABOUT MY LIFE. I CAN TELL
YOU I WAS BORN IN A SMALL TOWN AND LIVE IN ONE STILL. I
CAN TELL YOU I WAS A POLICE DETECTIVE HERE FOR TWENTY-
FIVE YEARS BEFORE I RETIRED. I CAN TELL YOU I'M STILL
OUT THERE EVERY DAY AND THAT CRAZY THINGS ARE STILL
HAPPENING.

I'LL LEAVE YOU WITH ONE QUESTION—IS ANY OF THIS TRUE?

JASON STRANGE
RAVENS PASS

Glossary

asphyxiation (az-fik-see-AY-shuhn)—suffocation

clenched (KLENCHD)—held or squeezed tightly

decaying (di-KAY-ing)—the rotting or breaking down of plant or animal matter

fatigued (fuh-TEEGD)—exhausted and weary

filthy (FILTH-ee)—dirty

frustrated (FRUHSS-tray-tid)—was made to feel helpless and discouraged

grimy (GRIME-ee)—sticky and dirty

groggily (GROG-uh-lee)—sleepily or dizzily

severance (SEV-ur-uhnss)—payment given to an employee after they have been released from employment

stumbling (STUHM-buhl-ing)—tripping, or walking in an unsteady way

1. Do you believe in ghosts? Why or why not?

2. What part of this story did you think was the scariest? Why?

3. Henry's new home creeped him out. Talk about times when you've been scared.

1. At what point in this story did you figure out that Henry was dead? Write down any clues or suspicious things you noticed about Henry and his mother.

2. The librarian doesn't believe Henry's story. Has an adult ever not believed what you had to say? Were you telling the truth? Write about what happened.

3. What happens to Henry and his mother after this story ends? Write a final chapter to this book.

for more

monsters
GHOSTS
secrets

JASON STRANGE

creatures

visit us at www.capstonepub.com